For Madison Mancini

No part of this publication may be reproduced, stored in a retrieval system, or transmitted in any form or by any means, electronic, mechanical, photocopying, recording, or otherwise, without written permission of the publisher. For information regarding permission, please write to: Permissions Department, Scholastic Inc., 557 Broadway, New York, NY 10012.

This book was originally published in hardcover by the Blue Sky Press in 2011.

ISBN 978-0-545-17533-3 (Trade) / ISBN 978-0-545-38580-0 (BC)

Be sure to check out Dav Pilkey's Extra-Crunchy Web Site O' Fun at www.pilkey.com.

12 11 10 9 8 7 6 5 4 3 2 1   11 12 13 14 15 16/0

Printed in the United States of America   40
First printing, September 2011

The EPIC Story Behind The EPIC Story of Super Diaper Baby

By George B. and Harold H.

Once upon a while ago, there were **2** Ridonk-ulous kids named George and Harold.

They dont get any awesom-er than us!!!

me too!

They wrote a amazing Book called the "Adventures of Super Diaper Baby."

But Unforchenetly, their mean Principel, Mr. Krupp read it.

Super Diaper Baby

It was the Story of a baby who acksidentLy fell into some super power JUice.

Splash

He drank it and got super Powers and stuff.

Also, a dog drank the Juice.

gLug Glug

He became super powery, too!

The Baby and the dog are best friends now and they Live Together with their mom and dad.

They both wear diapers too!

one time a evil guy tried to Steal Super Diaper Babys powers...

This is going to be sweet!

...but he made a boo-boo and got Turned into poo-poo!

Hey!

Transfer HeLMeT

Then he got some New clear waste on him and he grew way bigger and eviler!!!

Rar!

New clear power PLant

So Super Diaper Baby and Diaper Dog FLEW Into action!

We'll get you DepuTy Doo-Doo!

nuh-uh!!!

They grabbed a big Roll of ToiLeT paper from on Top of a bilding...

BOB's ToiLeT Paper compenY

HeY NO fair!

BoB

...wrapped up Deputy Doo-Doo...

...and Left him where all doo-doo belongs!

WELCOME TO URANUS

Hooray for super Diaper Baby and Diaper Dog!

So George and Harold read the book and got inspired and stuff.

So George and Harold starded creating their all-new epic Novel, Super Diaper Baby 2.

I bet MR. KRUPP WiLL be super happy!

me too!

They bet wrong.

What The---

This is even more offensiver Than your Last Book !!!

So thats The story of how super Diaper Baby 2 was invented.

DETENSHON

BiZZY WORK

BiZZY WORK

as usual, we hope you Like it more Than Mr. Krupp Did.

Chapters

Chapter 1
"A Day at the Park"

One day the Hoskins family went to the park for a picnick.

This looks like a nice spot.

sniff sniff

I will set up the picnick while you boys play.

What would you like to play, Billy?

me play airplane with Daddy.

Dad

14

WARNING

The following flip pages start out "cuteish", but get violentish (and even violentisher) as this novel goes along.

FLiPPER'S DiSGRESHON ADViSED

FLiP·O·RAMA

HEres How it works!!!!

STEP 1

Place your Left hand inside the dotted Lines marked "Left Hand Here". Hold the Book open FLAT.

STEP 2

GRasp the Right-hand Page with your Right thumb and index finger (inside the dotted Lines marked Right Thumb Here").

STEP 3

Now Quickly FLip the Right-hand Page back and fourth UnTiL the Pitcher appears to Be Animated!

(for extra fun, try adding your own Sound Afecks).

FLIP-O-RAMA #1

(pages 19 and 21)

Remember, Flip ONLY page 19. While you are Flipping, be shure you can see the Pitcher on page 19 AND the one on page 21.

IF you Flip Quickly, the two pitchers will start to Look Like one Animated Pitcher.

Dont forget to add your own Sound Afecks!

Left Hand Here

Down Goes the Airplane...

Right
thumb
Here

Up Goes the Airplane...

FLIP-O-RAMA 2

Remember---FLip **ONLY** page 23. While you are FLipping, be shure you can see the pitcher on page 23 **and** the one on page 25.

If you flip Quickly, The Two pitchers will start To Look Like one animated pitcher.

Don'T forget Those sound aFecks!

Left Hand Here

Down go the airplane

Right
Thumb
Here

Up go the airplane

Its OK, Son. It was a acksident.

Now Lets enjoy this nice Lunch that Mommy made.

BUT Then...

Hey Mister...

That big dumb bully Just stoled my doll. Will you help me?

I shure will!

Wait, Mr. HoSkins...

27

29

So the Hoskinses started to eat thier picnick lunch

BUT Then...

Hey mister...

Our ball got stuck up on the roof over there. Will you help us?

I shure will.

#1 Dad

Wait--- my daddy got hurted!

#1 Dad

Let super Diaper Baby handle this!

31

Finally the Hos-Kinses got BACK to finishing Thier Picnick Lunch.

BUT THEN...

Hey mister!

My son broke his Big Toe playing Kickball. Can you drive us To The hospitel?

I shure will !!!

Wait, Mr. Hoskins. That Will Take Forever !!!

That night at the Hoskinses House...

Honey, whats wrong?

Oh nothing... It's just...

Its hard having two Super Heros in the family.

Theyre better than me at everything!!!

I feel so... "ungood" at stuff.

34

I bet your still good at reading Bedtime Storys!

Oh yeah!

I almost forgot. Im awesome at That!!!

Im going To go do that Right now!

Oh Billy?

BILLYS Room

Knock KNOCK

Im am here to read you your faverite Bed-Time story!

Mecha-Frog and RobotoAd are enemys

No daddy. Me read to you Tonite!

Ha Ha! You cant read. Your Just a baby!

Actually, he can read. The super power juice he drank also made him super smart!!! He Taught himself To read this morning!

AND SO...

..."no," shouted Mecha Frog. "Not until you defeet my army of Ribbit Robots!".

36

This is Dr. Dilbert Dinkle and his evil cat, Petey. Dr. Dinkle is the one on the Left with the beard and the male-pattern Baldness. Petey is the one on the Right with the stripes and the tail.

Remember that, now!

Tonight we will **rob** This Bank using my new invenchon: The Liquidater 2000!

it Turns stuff into **WATER!!!**

It does this by rearanging molecules!

and Then---

You have Bad Breath.

40

SPLASH

uh oh!!!

BUT THEN...

I-I goT Turned into Water!!!

GRRRRR

43

No way! We came here to rob this bank and I'm not leaving without my cash!!!

Rats!

Bank Vault

Hmmm...

I ● know what to do!!!

Bank Vault

Sinse Im made out of water, I can flatten myself into a puddle and slide under the door!

45

Hey Petey! Grab a bag and start loading up this money...

Bank Vault

Ya dumb head!

Ewww! Its all wet!

1,000 USA 1,000 1,000 MOOLAH 1,000

Bank Vault

Thats a Y.P. not a M.P.

Later, in their Lair of Evil on top of Mount Cleveland...

Lair of Evil

Im RICH!!! Rich I tell you!

and you know what? I kinda like being made out of water!

It's totally easy to steal stuff...

PLUS, I can hide anywhere!!!

See, Petey? I look just like a puddle! You can't even see me, I bet!!!

I can still smell your breath, though!

So what??? I got super powers!

48

49

SO ANYWAYS...

The city turned our water off and I'm thirsty!!!

Thats a **YP**, Not a **MP**!

Well what am I suppost to Drink???

Listen, bub! I've been bizzy robbing banks all night! Quit Bugging me!

I'm going To sleep!

YAWN

AAAAAAh!

FLIP·O·RAMA 3

If you forgot how to do this already, please see your doctor. Afterwards, turn to page 17 for further instruckshons

Left Hand Here.

Drinking Dr. Dinkle

Right
Thumb
Here.

Drinking Dr. Dinkle

Lick
Lick
Lick
Lick
Lick

Lick
Lick
Lick
Lick

Lick
Lick
Lick
L'

AAAAh! That hit the spot!

now for a good nights sleep!

PETEY

ZZZZZ

PETEY

6 Hours Later...

Lair of evil

58

60

CHAPTER 3
Daddy DiLema

Left Hand Here.

Snatcher Catchers

63

Right Thumb Here

Snatcher Catchers

How come Daddy don't feel important?

I'm not shure... I just don't think he feels very Brave or strong compared to us.

after all, we're super heros and he isn't.

Help! That Guy just stoled my car!!!

Haw Haw

FLiP-O-RAMA 5

Left Hand Here

Jacker Smackers

Right
Thumb
Here

Jacker Smackers

FLIP-O-RAMA 6

Left Hand Here

Cheater Beaters!

Right thumb Here

Cheater Beaters!

I can't believe it! I went to sleep and when I woke up, I got turned into pee!

Hey, I should call you "Rip Van Tinkle!"

You Better not!!!

Alright, Rip Van Tinkle. I won't.

YOUR in BIG TROUBLE!!!

Doncha mean "Urine" Big Trouble?

It's not funny!!! My whole body got turned into pee!!!

Hey! Maybe you'll win a Peebody Award!!!

AAAAAUGH!!!!!!!
I cant stand it!!!
Im going to go
do some shopping!

Hey Rip
van
Tinkle,
can I
come?

NO!!!
And quit calli-
ng me
That!!!

Lair
of Evil

AND SO...

Knock-Knock

77

78

79

sniff
sniff

Ye Old
BLing
Shoppe

open

You get out of my store!

Ye OLd
BLing
Shoppe

open

How come?

ya got
Pee aLL
over every-
thing!!!

But Lookit all The money I Got!!!

Too Bad! It smells Like Pee!

Your moneys no good here!!!

Ye OL
BLi
Shop

SLAM

closed

Fine!!! ILL go someplase ELse then!!

Chapter 4 (Part 2)

How The Pee Stoled Potties!

By
Dr. George
and
Dr. Harold

That Night Rip Van Tinkle
was frowning a frown,
as he sneered at the houses
below in the town.

No one knows why he was
feeling so ruthless...
It could be because all his
money was useless.

86

Or maybe because he was
just feeling cranky.
Or possibly cuz his bad breath
was so stanky.
But we think the very best
reason might be
that he smelled like a bucket
of twelve-day-old pee.

But whatever the reason
his stank or his dough,
he stood up there hating
the people below.
He snarled as he frowned
feeling drearier and drearier.
"Those Jerks in the city
Think Theyr'e so superier!

88

"They all be hatin´!
   But heres what I think:
I think things would change
   if they started to stink!

If all of those idiots
   smelled just like pee,
they wouldent be goin´ Round
disrespectin´ me!!!

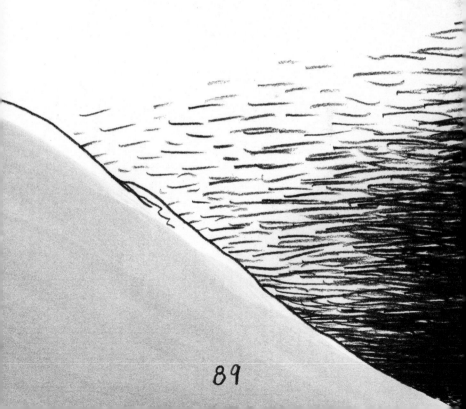

And then Rip Van Tinkle
   Thought up a idea.
But we couldent Think up
   a rhyme for "idea".

"I Know just what to do"
   he started professin'.
"I'LL teach all of those good-
   smelling people a Lessen!"

So he Took Some scrap metal
and used an old wheel
To build a contrapshon
with Teeth made of steel.

He hammered its tail
and sharpened its claws,
and welded its wiskers
and titened its Jaws.

93

It took 24 hours
  From when he'd begun,
'Till the Robo-Kitty
  Three Thousand was done.
"ALL I need is a driver.
  I need someone mean.
I need someone evil
  to run my machine".

So he took his cat "Petey"
  and strapped him in tight...

...Then both of those villens sneaked out in the night.

"Watch this," Rip Van Tinkle said
Laffing out Loud...
and soon he began to
Turn into a Cloud.

And when the pee cloud
was over the town,
the thunderclaps crashed
and the pee drops rained down.

Into the chimneys
the pee drops they flew
And they entered each house
Knowing just what to do.

Each drop found a wrench...

... and each wrench found a bolt...

JOLT

...and soon every toilet popped up with a JOLT!

They carried each toilet
    Right out of each house, and
Into the jaws of the
    Kitty Three thousend.

Crunch! crunch! went the robot
without too much trouble
and soon every potty
was crushed into rubbel!

But in one little house,
   on one little street,
One drip heard the sounds
   of two little feet.

The pee drop looked up
   and what did it see?
but a cute little tot
   with a fluffy blankie.

The baby looked down
and said, "MR. Pee, Hey!
Why are you taking
our toilet away?"

And that mean little drip,
do you know what it did?
Why, it made up a lie
and it said to the kid:

"Your toilet is broken---
it squeaks when you flush it.
I'll take it away and I'll
clean it and brush it.

I'll shine it right up
—I'll fix it and oil it,
and soon I'll return with a
Good-as-new toilet."

And the baby believed what
the pee drop had said.
So it got him a juice box
and took him to bed.

And at last when the baby
was sleeping and dreaming,
that nasty old pee drop
went on with its skeeming!

He carried The Toilet
Right out the door.
and once it was crushed,
He went back to get more.

The snatching of Potties
went on through the night,
And into the dawn of the
Mornings first Light.

And Once Every Toilet
was crushed by the cat,
The people awoke and cried,
"What up wit' dat?"

"Our toilets are gone!
  Weve got to go Potty!
Oh, we do not Like this!
  Oh, no we do notty!"

So they each crossed their legs
and squirmed all around,
And they squeezed and they clenched,
and they bobbed up and down.

'Till all of the people
were doing "pee dances"
shouting, "someone please help us,
or we'll wet our pantses!"

They wiggled all morning
in torment and Trauma,
Just Like they're doing
in this FLip-o-Rama →

Left Hand
Here

Pee-Dance
RevoLushon

Right
Thumb
Here

Pee-Dance
RevoLushon

Soon, warm liquid streams
with yellowish Hues
Flowed down their Legs
and filled up their Shoes.

And they sobbed as they stood
in their puddles of piddle,
But no one could help them.
Not even a little.

CHAPTER 5

the Aftermath

Soon the mornful cries of a thousend Pants-Peeing People reached the evil ears of Petey and the Pee Drops.

Waaaaa!

Hey fellas! Lets Join Back Together!

OK!

The Last one in is a roten egg!

So what's the next part of our evil Plan?

next ParT?

Yeah, You Know, what are we gonna do **Next**???

um... I dont Know. Wanna watch a movie or something?

That WASnt your **WHOLE PLAN**, was it?

What?

Are you saying we went through ALL That trouble Just so people would wet their pants and smell like pee?

umm... Kinda.

AAAAUGH!

That's the **DUMBEST** Evil Plan I ever Heard of!

Well if your so smart, why dont you think up a evil Plan!!!

OK, I WILL!!!

Hmmm... Let me think...

NoBody has a toilet anymore...

Everybody has to go Pee-Pee...

I Got it!!!

124

BUT THEN

We interupt this show to tell you some importent stuff!!!

5 Action News

As you all know, everybodys toilet got stoled last night.

5 Action News

Nobody has a plase to pee anymore so the mayor has drained the city's pool...

Please feel free to pee in this empty pool until our crisis is resolved!

Local kids had this to say:

This is Awesome!

I've been peeing in that pool for years! Now I dont have to feel gilty!

me too!

in other news, a Giant Robotic cat is stealing all the citys diapers!

⑤ action news

Its going from store to store taking every diaper in town!!!

Diaper Depot

SALE

who will save us from this madness???!?

This looks like a job for us!

Hooray!

EXTEND
-O-TAiL

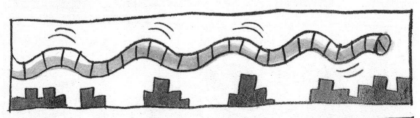

CLICK!

VRRRR!

Ka-ching!

133

TA·SHMMM

Q·KUN

K·LiK

K·LOK

MMMM

P·FUT

K·CHUNK

P·KAF

T·SHING

O·PRAH

chi-BAFF

P-KRANG

140

Left
Hand Here

Koo-Koo For Kitty Nip!

Right thumb Here

Koo-Koo For Kitty Nip!

FLIP·O·RAMA

Left Hand Here

KItty FOR KOO-KOO NiP!

Right thumb Here.

KiTTY FOR KOO-KOO NiP!

150

CHAPTER 6

The Revenge of Rip Van Tinkle

mayor! mayor!

Everybody in Town has been Peeing in the Pool all day Long!!!

Thats wonderful!!!

But sir, the Pool is filled to the top with Pee! shoudent we drain it???

non-sence my Good man!

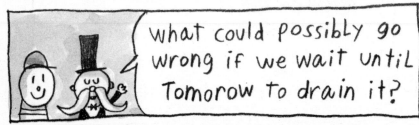

what could possibly go wrong if we wait until Tomorow to drain it?

153

I Live AGAin!

155

FLiP-O-RAMA

Left Hand Here

Building Basher

Right
thumb
Here

Building Basher

Remember back a Long Time ago when me was really Little?

You mean Last week?

Yeah!

Well, remember when me put me's Juice Box in the freezer on acksident?

Heh-Heh! Yeah, it Froze Solid!

Hey!!! Your idea Just gave me a idea!!!

Push down on the ground, Billy! Push as hard as you can!!!

Billy and Diaper Dog pushed and pushed...

...and slowly things began to move.

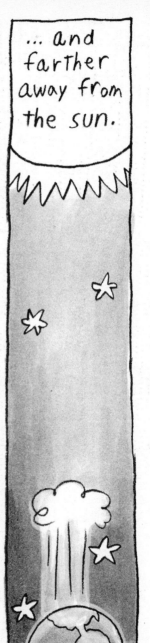

171

ALL we have to do now...

...is wrap this rope around him...

...and Take him to a planet where he will never melt!

Where?

Why uranus of course!!!

But on the way, Billy got another good idea!

wisper
wisper
wisper

172

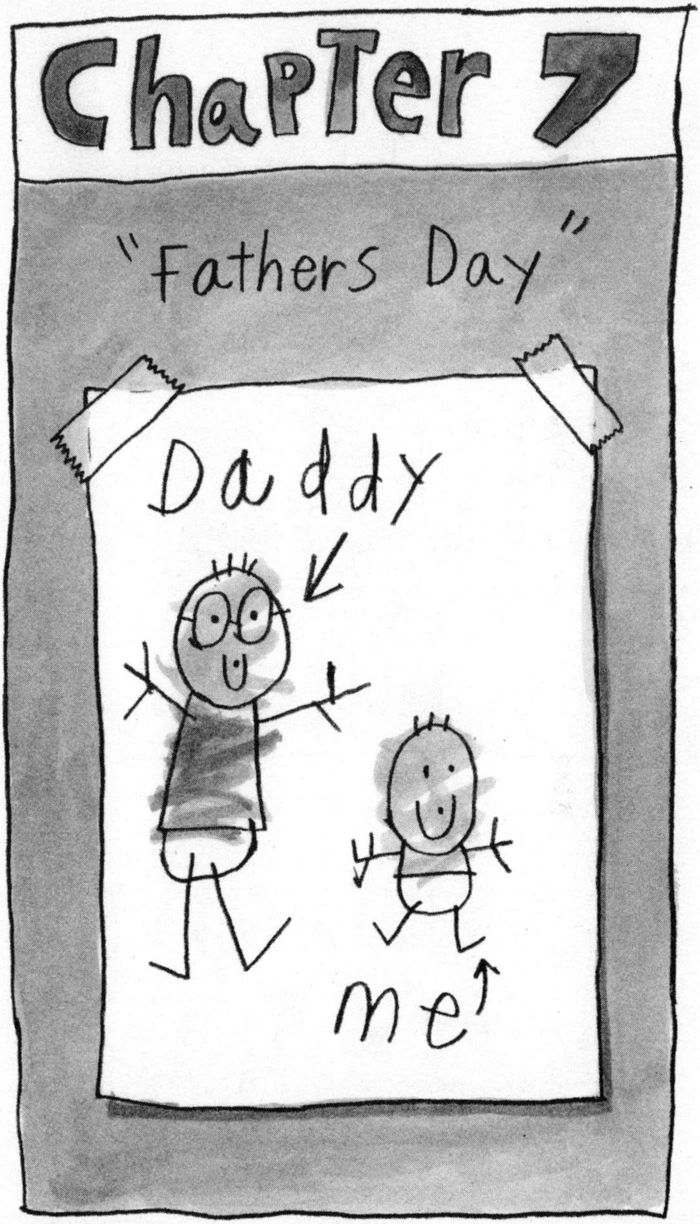
ChapTer 7
"Fathers Day"
Daddy
me

Meanwhile at the Hoskinses House...

I'm am so worried about Billy and Diaper Dog!!! where could they be?

I don't Know sweat Heart.

BOOM

Hi momma and Daddy!

BILLY!

Daddy Theres a big Ice monster Outside!!!

Im so glad your safe!!!

Daddy Look at the ice monster!!

OK, OK. Lets Look at this silly ice monster of yours!

ILL JUST open these curtins and take a peek!

175

Umm... Well, I wish you wouldent do that.

Why not???

Because, um... its not very nice.

Well what are you Gonna do about it, huh?

Umm... Umm...

me shure is proud of you, daddy! your super brave!!!

really?

183

Then Billy and Diaper Dog moved the Earth back to its proper place in space...

...and flew back home to join the celebrashon!

Hey it stopped snowing!

Can I take a pitcher of the Hero Dad for our newspaper?

OK

Hooray!!!

Left Hand Here.

Say Cheese!!!

Right
thumb
Here

Say Cheese!!!

READ GEORGE AND HAROLD'S FIRST TWO EPIC ADVENTURES!

Faster than a speeding stroller, more powerful than diaper rash, and able to leap tall buildings without making poopy-stinkers, it's Super Diaper Baby!

"Readers... will revel in the humor." —Kirkus Reviews

"All the kid-tickling silliness that fans... can't get enough of." —Publishers Weekly

Meet Ook and Gluk, the two coolest caveboys to step out of the Stone Age!

"Completely immature... completely hilarious.... Destined to fly off the shelves." —School Library Journal

"Pilkey continues to offer the exact goofy, quirky details that [readers] will find perfect." —The Bulletin of the Center for Children's Books

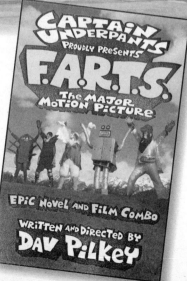